BWWM
Kathleen Hope

Table Of Contents

Prologue: The Beginning of a Lifetime. 3
Chapter One: A Far Throw 7
Chapter Two: Striking Out 11
Chapter Three: Finally a Hit 15
Epilogue: The Perfect Game 20
Bonus Sample: The Ride Of Her Life 25
Extra Bonus Sample: Flames Of Passion 35

Prologue: The Beginning of a Lifetime.

Andrew Bernholz had loved baseball since the first time he had picked one up at the age of only five. As his tiny hand came around the lacing of the leather bound ball, he felt something within him ignite. It was like the first moment that a writer picks up a pen or a ballet dancer wears their first slippers. It was like his destiny was chosen from the very first moment that the ball left his hand. He remembered the warm summer day vividly. In fact, it was the happiest memory that he held onto. He and his father played catch in the front yard of their family home. His mother was inside making apple pie and vanilla ice cream, his favorite. His father showed him how to throw a fastball, a wind up, and also, his favorite, a changeup. After that, his father showed him how to bat. He showed him how to get behind the plate, steady his knees, and aim for the back gate. At the time, the back gate was just a tree that was about 5 feet away and in a real field it's about 725 feet away. Andrew worked for the rest of his life to hit the backfield gate. Even though Andrew was a fantastic batter, he preferred pitching, it was his strong suit. There was just something about standing on the mound, with the sun in your eyes, with your hat tipped forward, surrounded by dirt. There was a certain silence that came over the crowd before the pitch happened. There was a certain tension in the air, and Andrew loved every bit of it. He felt like he was on center stage doing something worth watching. Newspapers and bloggers showed up to talk about all of the potential that Andrew was capable of. Coaches from other teams would do everything that they could to convince Andrew to join their teams, including basketball, football and soccer, hoping that his talent would carry over and make their teams as great as the baseball team. Even though he did well at these other sports, no other one would ever take away from his love of baseball. Everything else came second. He learned so many things just from a baseball, a bat, and glove. He learned how to respect his coaches and how to appreciate all of his teammates. The things that he learned on that field would be some of the most important lessons he ever learned.

Andrew spent so many hours of his day standing in front of a return net. He would throw his best ball and it would bounce back to him, ready to try again. Over and over again he practiced different throws, perfecting his pitch. Where the other children saw tedious and obnoxious practicing workouts Andrew saw his nirvana. He would watch as the ball left his hand and made contact in the direct middle of the white taped square that marked the average strike zone. The net would cave under the force that he delivered through the ball. He would critique every spin and each roll, making each and every one better than the last.

After his parents got divorced, when he was only 10, the baseball field was the only place and he had ever felt truly at home. He felt like all the boys in the dugout were his brothers. He felt like the coach was his father. After his father left, he never saw too much of him, maybe once or twice a month. His coach, Randy Watson however, was always around. He would come for late night dinners, bringing mother and him some wonderful food and great company. He would also teach Andrew some great pointers in that same front yard and they would pay catch. They would talk about all of the on goings in school and in life. They would talk about what Andrew wanted to do as he got older. His answer had always been the same: professional baseball player. With the way Andrew played it wasn't a totally irrational dream. In fact, everyone in Greensprings believed that he could do it. He'd been the best to ever play at the high school or at the local college. There was so much determination inside of him; there was nothing that he allowed to stop him. If he wanted to be a professional baseball player then he was going to be a professional baseball player.

That dream had finally begun to become a reality one day in May. Andrew sat on the pitcher's mound, the way that he always had. He adjusted the ball in his fingers so that his pointer, middle and index finger held on tightly but his wrist was loose. The game so far had been what was called a "no-hitter". It only happens when the pitcher strikes out each and every single batter. There was a scout in the audience for the Colorado Rockies. Everyone knew so everyone was playing their best. Still, that didn't stop Andrew from playing the best game of his life. He threw the ball, it flew right over home plate, and the batter didn't swing. The umpire, dressed in a blue polo shirt and khakis, stood up and screamed the best words that a pitcher can hear.

"Strike three! You're out!" The umpire yelled as he stood up and held up his hands.

Andrew's team ran to him, yelling out his name. They picked him up into their arms and yelled with joy. Andrew looked out to the crowd as they cheered and threw their fists into the air. The newspaper took pictures and shouted the headlines that would captivate the entire town. Andrew watched for the reaction of the Rockies' scout carefully. The man that was dressed so well pulled out a cell phone with a smile and called whomever he had needed to. After all of the commotion calmed down, the man came to Andrew. His heart clenched as he got closer and closer.

"How would you like to play for the Colorado Rockies, son?"

Chapter One: A Far Throw

It had been five years since Andrew had been signed to the Colorado Rockies. It had been so long in fact, that it had come for the day for him to retire. That made today his most important game. No pitcher wants to go out losing his last game. Andrew had it in his mind that he was going to throw a perfect game, a game just like the game that got him signed to the Rockies. Andrew focused on the pitch. As he wound up, out of the corner of his eye he caught a glimpse of most beautiful woman he ever seen. She was taller than most women, but she was also the most beautiful woman he had ever seen. Her hair was long and curly. Her face was defined and her body was something to be admired and worshiped. Her dark chocolate complexion seemed to sparkle from the sun. She was jumping up-and-down, holding a sign with Andrew's name. Andrew had not realized it until everyone in the crowd gasped, but he had literally dropped the ball. In confusion, the umpire called it a ball. That put an end to Andrew's perfect game.

 The game ended and people gave their condolences to Andrew. Most people knew how important it had been for him. He walked out the field and began looking for the woman that he had seen, the one that had distracted him from his perfect game. She was the most beautiful woman he had ever seen. He returned to the dugout and sat on the bench. He was going to miss being the center of attention in a huge stadium like this one. When you're a pitcher you wear out your pitching arm exceptionally fast. It's such an unnatural motion for the body to move in, especially on an almost daily basis. Regardless of how much he took care of it the damage had been done. And now, what did he have to show for it? A botched game. Of course, his game had been a victory, just not to the extent that he had anticipated. He pulled his hat over his eyes and looked at all of the sunflower seeds strewn across the concrete underneath the bleachers. He leaned his head back and looked up. Of course, he could always go and watch his teammate's games. He knew the team would move on without him, but he was stuck, stranded without them. His entire life was baseball and now that he didn't have it he didn't know what to do. He felt like he was completely lost. What is one supposed to do after they complete their lifelong dream? He had never really filled his thoughts with anything but baseball before. He had never had any other hobbies or interests, just baseball. The only thought that ever crossed his mind besides baseball was the woman that he'd seen today. He began to think of every way that he could possibly meet her. He was equal parts serious and curious about her. Women threw themselves at him on an almost daily basis. He was used to being the center of attention of models and actresses. He never felt the way about them that he felt about her. She caught his eye, instead of vice versa. He knew that she was a fan; he just had to figure out how to get in touch with his fan.

Andrew had always loved his fans, but he never spent much time with them. He never wanted to chat or talk to them as he signed autographs. That's not to say that he wasn't kind to them, because he very much was. His mind was always just so focused on other things. He knew that without his fans he would have no franchise or career. The thing about professional baseball is that it's just as much about the fans as it is about the talent; although, he didn't have to worry about any of that anymore. Tonight, he would return to his mansion, eat dinner, probably from sort of savory pot roast. Then, he would probably crawl into his bed and wonder some more about what he was going to do with the rest of his life. That was the thought that the news caster was interested in when she brought the microphone to Andrew's mouth.

"I'm sorry, I'm late." She said. "I'm sure you don't want to talk, and I'm sure the bigger stations already got all the good stuff, but, would you mind?"

"I don't mind." Andrew said as he stood up and straightened out his clothing.

"That was some game." The newscaster said with a smile.

"I was distracted." Andrew said, getting a little bit frustrated.

"What was it that distracted you?" The woman asked.

Andrew thought about it. This was going to be the way that he got back in touch with the woman, the way that he reached out to her and got a hold of her. He stood in front of the camera with his back straight.

"Actually, a woman is to blame. She was a beautiful woman. She was wearing one of my jerseys and she had long black hair and the most beautiful eyes that I've ever seen. Any lead on the responsible woman would be highly appreciated." Andrew said with a wink as he gave his number. Almost immediately his phone began to ring.

"Are you serious?" The newscaster asked laughing.

"As serious as throwing the perfect retirement game." Andrew said.

The woman shut off the camera and looked at Andrew.

"Do you know how many replies you're going to get because of that?" She said with a laugh.

"It will be worth it." He said back as he screened calls.

The woman wasn't wrong. It had only been a few hours since Andrew had announced his phone number on live TV and already he had more than one hundred calls. No more would be accepted. Andrew began to call the people that had called him.

Chapter Two: Striking Out

Over 1,000 phone calls came in over the next month. Unfortunately, none of them ended the way Andrew had wanted them to. None of them led him to the woman that had distracted him from the game. He had done everything he could. He had posted on every main social media site, he had returned all of the phone calls, and he had even searched the cameras. He was beginning to give up hope that he was ever going to find the woman again. He was not even sure that she wanted to be found anyway. He was beginning to give up hope when a phone call finally came in.

"Did the woman you saw have dark skin and blue eyes?" The man on the other line asked. Andrew was put off by his old smoker's cough. The man sounded like he was up to no good. Not like he wanted money, just like he wasn't supposed to know about this woman. Andrew couldn't help but to be bit skeptical of the man. He sounded like he was in his late 70's and trying to hide something that he didn't want Andrew to know. Still, he thought that it was worth it to comply. He'd come this far there was no use in stopping it now.

"As a matter of fact she did." Andrew said, intrigued.

"Do you have an email that I can send you a picture of my daughter? I think you may have been talking about her." The man asked. Andrew thought it was a little strange.

"Yes." He replied skeptically. Andrew continued to name off his email address to the strange man. Ten minutes later, he received the picture. It was a picture of a beautiful woman. She had been much younger in the photos than when Andrew had seen her at the game, but it was definitely her. She was absolutely stunning too. She was in a short white summer dress and held a stack of books. She wore a big, beautiful smile on her angelic face. "You said this is your daughter?" Andrew asked in awe that he was looking at her again. He had wanted for so long to see her again, and now there she was on the computer screen, more beautiful than he remembered. As he looked into her deep blue eyes, he realized that he never wanted to look into anyone else's eyes for as long as he lived. She was the vision of perfection and he was willing to do whatever he could to see her again. Unfortunately, that was at the will of the man on the phone. He didn't sound like he was a reasonable man to deal with and this was a sensitive matter, that, if taken into the wrong hands could be easily taken advantage of. Andrew failed to think of any other way that the man could have known about this woman if he hadn't been telling the god's honest truth.

"Yes, that's my little Natasha. That's the last picture I have of her. After she went to college she kind of cut me out of her life. I still know where she is, but I can't go near her. That's where I was hoping that you could come in. I want to get back in touch with my daughter and you can help me with that. If you agree, I can point you in the right direction of her." The man said. Andrew could tell from his voice that he was being sincere but it was still a strange request nonetheless. He didn't know this man at all, he could be some type of sociopath and not really know her.

"Sir, if you ask me, I think that if she wants you in her life, that she'll let you in her life." Andrew said respectfully, not wanting to upset or anger the old man. He sounded distressed enough. A thousand and one situations ran through his head as to why Natasha would want to keep him out of her life. Andrew's father was known to mess up pretty badly, but never bad enough to where Andrew wanted to kick him out of his life entirely. In fact, he couldn't imagine his father doing something vile enough to warrant such a thing as that. A child's love for their parent is unconditional even when a parent's may not be. Andrew weighed his options.

"Well, what says that she wants you in her life? You went on a national news broadcast about her. I think it's safe to say that neither of us is exactly taking the high road, but I was hoping you'd understand." The man said.

"I'm not a hypocrite, so I guess I'll help you." Andrew said. "What's your plan?"

"She lives in a tiny apartment with her roommates. I can give you the address and then what you do with it is up to you. I just want you to convince her to come back and at least talk to me." The man said.

He gave Andrew the address. Andrew went straight to his computer to confirm it. Sure enough it came back as the home of Natasha Green. Andrew then began to plot and to think about how he was going to woo her. He didn't want it to feel like he just showed up at her house, uninvited. It took him over a week, but Andrew finally had the perfect idea in mind on how to win over Natasha.

Chapter Three: Finally a Hit

Andrew walked up to the small apartment. He heard what must have been at least five women inside laughing and enjoying each other's company. Andrew stood there with a dozen roses hoping that one of them was Natasha. He knocked on the door with a large smile on his face. He held his breath as a woman opened the door. The woman wasn't Natasha, but she was around her age. Andrew smiled as a bewildered look came across her face.

"Is Natasha Green here?" Andrew asked.

The woman's eyes got even bigger. Andrew was dressed in a very expensive suit. He had his hair slicked back, the way that he got the most compliments on it. The woman stuttered as she tried to speak.

"I'm sorry, she's not here. Who are you?" The woman asked.

"I'm Andrew Bernholz, former Rockies pitcher. Natasha was at my last game. I was hoping that I would be able to speak to her." Andrew answered.

The woman took a moment to gain her mind back before she spoke. She looked down at all that Andrew held.

"I don't think that you're going about it the right way. If you want to speak to Natasha, she's going to be extremely put off by this." The young woman motioned to Andrew from head to toe. "If there's one thing that you need to know about Natasha, it's that she doesn't enjoy dramatic acts. You're going to have tone it down."

"Thank you for the advice," Andrew said, feeling embarrassed. "Can you please point me in her direction?

"Of course," The woman said. She began to write down the address of a bar on Main Street.

Andrew drove as his stomach clenched into a knot. His heart began to flutter as he watched the bar come into view. He parked his car and walked through the front doors. He sat the roses beside him as he took a seat at the bar. A man dressed in tight pants and a plaid shirt walked up to him.

"What will it be?" The man asked as he cleaned out a glass with a white rag.

"I'll take a rum and Coke, also, can you point me in the direction of Natasha?" Andrew asked. The man looked him over before nodding.

"Here's your rum and Coke. Wait here." The man disappeared behind a curtain. The moments that it took for the curtain to flutter back open made him feel like he waited there for an eternity. Finally, Natasha stepped in front of him. She dropped the tray of glasses that she was holding when she looked at his face.

"Oh my God, Andrew Bernholz, what are you doing here?" She asked.

"Actually, I came here to see you." Her mouth dropped open. "Are you okay?" Andrew asked.

"Why would you come all the way here just to see me?" She asked with her hands still up to her face.

"Haven't you been watching TV?" Andrew asked.

"I don't have one." She said as she laughed and swept up the broken glass.

"Well, you're the reason why I didn't throw a perfect game. My retirement game, you were there." Andrew said making sure to be as sweet as possible about it. He didn't want to upset her.

"Me?" She said with her eyes wide. "I am so sorry, what did I do?"

"When I saw you I couldn't take my eyes off you. I couldn't keep them on the ball." He said. "Which is pretty much the first rule of baseball."

"Oh, I am so sorry." She said about to cry.

"No, please don't be upset. After I saw you, you're all that I could think about." As Andrew said it, he felt the same overwhelming emotion that took him over when he very first picked up a baseball. She took her hand back and held it to her chest.

"You're not angry?" She asked innocently.

"No, of course I'm not. However, I will be broken if you deny me a dinner date tonight, at the *Blue Moon*." Andrew said with his lady killer grin.

"Of course, I'll go." Natasha said as she looked into Andrew's eyes. Andrew sat at the bar as he enjoyed Natasha's conversation and a few virgin drinks. He admired her astonishing body from her beautiful hair to her large breasts, down to her thick hips and her long legs. Andrew was exceptionally drawn in by her thick, plump lips that he loved to make curl into the most beautiful smile that he had ever seen. He realized that just being able to spend these few hours talking to her was worth it to have missed out on throwing a no hitter for his retirement game. When her shift ended, Andrew drove her back to her apartment so that she could get ready for their date. He frantically called his assistant while he was inside, making reservations for the *Blue Moon* Restaurant. Even men like Andrew had a hard time getting into the restaurant, especially on such short notice, but he put everything that he could into the night. He pulled string after string, and called in favors all because he wanted Natasha to feel what he felt for her.

Natasha came out of her front door looking extravagant. She wore a long red gown that would have dragged the ground if she hadn't kept it in her hand. She wore her long hair into a tight and curly bun that sat on top of her head perfectly. Her makeup had been changed from what she wore before. It was more elegant and sultry. Andrew had finished his call before she glided into the car like the goddess that she was. Andrew admired each and every movement that she danced. He loved the way that she tilted her head back and closed her delightful eyes in joy. It was utterly intoxicating.

Andrew was pleased as they arrived at the *Blue Moon*. He was overjoyed to see that all of his requests had been catered to. The couple had their own waitress and their own balcony table. They sat down, ready to enjoy a gourmet meal. Natasha smiled as Andrew told her all of the wonderful adventures that he had on his journey to becoming a professional baseball player. All of the arrogance that came along with the title that he held drifted away, and it just became an occupation as she listened with her smile.

"How did you find me?" Natasha asked after he finished speaking.

Epilogue: The Perfect Game

"I've been meaning to tell you that, actually. Your father contacted me. He saw the newscast and told me where I could find you." The look that came over her face was perturbed. "Our deal was that he would tell me where you were if I got you to talk to him. "

"I'm not surprised at all that he would do something like that. The reason why I've been estranged from him for so long is because he's an alcoholic. My entire childhood he always talked about how he had a disease. But the truth was that he decided to pick up each and every drink that he saw." Natasha said. Her face contorted into one of sorrow. "He spent the money for my mom's funeral on whiskey."

Andrew understood what it was like to have issues with his parents. He wanted to only make her feel better, but he also wanted to hold up his end of the bargain. He was a man of his word.

"What if he's changed? You don't want to miss that over something that happened in the past do you?" Andrew asked.

"Okay, I guess I do owe him something since he got us together." Natasha said.

After dinner, Natasha directed Andrew to her father's house. It was dilapidated and decaying. A wretched smell came from the house. Andrew held her hand as they walked up to the door. He watched her take a deep breath as she knocked. The man that opened the door was much older than Andrew would have thought that he would be for Natasha's father. He was gaunt, it looked like he had not eaten in almost a month. His skin was covered from head to toe with liver spots. He slouched at an angle, like a large weight had hung across his frail neck for a long time. However, he smiled as he saw Natasha.

"My baby girl!" He yelled as he took his daughter into his arms. At first, she struggled. Then, she eventually wrapped her arms around his thin frame too. "I'm off the hard stuff." He said. Andrew could see the relief in Natasha's eyes as he said it.

"Then why do you look this way, dad?" She asked.

"Drinking is an expensive habit." He answered. A look of shame came across his face while a look of pride came across Natasha's. "I'm sorry Tasha." He said sincerely.

Natasha's father welcomed Natasha and Andrew into his home as he thanked Andrew for holding up his end of their deal. Andrew watched as Natasha began to love, trust and forgive her father again. The sight was beautiful and rare. As Natasha excused herself to the restroom, Andrew sat next to her father who wore a wide smile. His eyes were grateful.

"Sir, I need you to know something. I love Natasha, and I want nothing more than to marry her, but I need your blessing. I see the way that she looks at you and I know that it took a long time, but I know that she cares about you and I know that she cares about what you think." Andrew said. Her father sighed.

"Yes. I wouldn't want anyone else more than you to be my son in law Andrew. I'd be honored." He said as he wrapped his arms around him.

Natasha came from the bathroom to see the two of them sitting next to each other laughing. She looked at them with happiness. She had never seen the way that a man was supposed to treat a woman until she met Andrew. Her father had always been too drunk to pay any attention to her mother; if he had maybe he would have noticed her cancer symptoms. She believed that she could find it in her heart to forgive him. She had always believed that he loved alcohol more than her, but, today he proved otherwise.

"Andrew, it's getting late." She said with a smile. Andrew nodded and grabbed his keys before taking Natasha's arm in his and leading her out to the car. Natasha kissed her father goodbye and promised to see him the next day. As they drove, Natasha noticed that Andrew wasn't driving back to the house. He comforted her by telling her that it was a surprise. She watched as they drove out of town and into the parking lot of the Rockies stadium. Andrew opened her door for her as

Natasha admired the empty lot and the empty stadium. Andrew pulled out a ring of keys and unlocked the entrance. The two of them walked onto the silent, dark field. All that lit up the sky was the stars above and the full moon. Andrew walked her out to the pitching mound.

"Since I was young this has been my life. It was like the moment I stepped on this mound I was the only person that existed. That changed on that last game. When I saw you it was like you were the only one who existed. I want to exist together." Andrew got down on one knee and pulled out a velvet box. He presented it to Natasha with begging eyes. "Will you marry me Natasha Green?"

"Do you know why I was your fan Andrew?" She asked, taking Andrew by surprise.

"No, why?" He asked.

"Because, you had all this talent, money and power, but I could tell that wasn't what you loved about the game. You were so different than the other men of the field. You loved the game; you were faithful to only a ball, and a bat, not to the women that came with it, or the fame or the cash. I never had a man to look up to in my life but that changed when I saw the very first Rockies game that you played. To see you put this game that you love so much second to me, means so much. So, yes Andrew, I will marry you."

THE END

I Need Your Help...

Thank you for purchasing this book!

I hope you enjoyed it and found it entertaining.

If you enjoyed this book, then I'd like to ask you for a favor. Could you be so kind to leave a positive review for this book on Amazon? It'd be greatly appreciated!

I want to reach as many people as I can with this book, and more reviews will help me accomplish that.

Not only that, you will get some good karma.

Thank you for your time and best wishes to you!

Bonus Sample: The Ride Of Her Life

June pulled up to the ranch in a Ford Sedan feeling entirely out of place. She hadn't really been around this sort of rural environment since she was a kid, but it was time to get the hell out of the city. So here she was. An old man who could have been her grandfather walked out of the house.

"You must be June."

"Yes, sir." She gave him a smile.

"I'm Roger." He eyed the car a moment then gestured her inside, out of the blazing heat that baked her skin as soon as she stepped out of the air conditioned car.

Squinting as she stepped into the more dimly lit house, June looked around, reminded all the more of her grandparents place and summers as a kid. He led her to the kitchen.

"So I understand you know how to work with horses? Got experience, you said. " He grumbled.

"Yes sir. I haven't done it in a long time, but I'm glad for the opportunity to do so again." June brushed her hair back. "I used to spend my summers on my grandparents ranch and my dad had some horses too. Mostly for show though."

"Just decided to get out of the city?" he asked. "Tea?"

"Yes, please. And it was time. I missed being out in the country like this. I appreciate the opportunity you're giving me, sir."

He poured her a glass of iced tea and looked her over. "Finish that and I'll introduce you to my grandson. He's the main one I have working with the horses, but I think it'll help him to have another hand around. Besides, I want to see how you do."

"Of course," she said. "Thank you." She finished the tea fairly quickly, aware of him watching her and wondering if that had been a test too as she handed the empty glass back and he put it in the sink.

They walked back outside and past a small garden. "If you get the job, there's an old bunkhouse you can stay in," he said, pointing to a ramshackle building next to the barn. She idly wondered if it even met safety codes.

"No problem," she replied.

He gave a small grunt in response and led her to the corral where a man only a couple years older than herself was walking a horse. "Harlan, this is that girl I was telling you about."

Harlan looked up at her and June was struck by his dark hair and blue eyes. "You're here to work the horses?" he asked, just a hint of condescension to his voice.

"Yep," June smiled, ignoring the tone.

He clucked at the horse and brought it to a stop. "Let's see what you can do," he said. Harlan walked the horse over to the corral and let it loose before going to the barn and taking out another horse. This one had a bit of a wild look in its eye, its mane and coat a dark black, with a crackle of white on its nose. *Good,* thought June, *perfect way to prove I can handle a horse.*

"This one here is Lightning," said Harlan.

"Unbroken, right? Okay." June slipped into the corral and took the lead. Harlan stepped back, but not out. The horse looked her over and started to pull away with a decisive snort. June spoke low and didn't let him walk away. With another soft command she got him to start walking, going slowly in a circle. He pulled away from her a few more times, but she kept him going, not letting him take control away from her.

June was happy to realize this felt like breathing, or maybe riding a bicycle. She'd been reading up on the subject since she'd decided to find a job and it was paying off now. Suddenly the horse went at her instead of pulling. She gave it a firm command and didn't back away, getting it back to the walking it had been doing. Out of the corner of her eye she saw the two men share a look.

"That's enough, June," said Roger, nodding to Harlan.

Still looking a bit unhappy about the whole situation, Harlan took the horse back from her.

"Come on, June, let's go over the paperwork and get you settled."

"Thank you, sir," she said. "Nice to meet you, Harlan."

He gave her half a nod and focused on the horse. June followed Roger back into the house. "He'll relax," he said. "Sometimes I think Harlan is as skittish as some of our horses. You just keep handling the horses right and he'll come around."

"Thank you." She sat at the table he gestured to and brought out some paperwork.

June read it over. Everything was like they'd agreed on over the phone. The pay wasn't great, but with somewhere to sleep it was making up for some of it. When she finished, she drove her car up to the ramshackle bunk house and stepped inside.

It wasn't quite so awful inside, but it still needed work. At least there was a bathroom and running water. "You can eat with us in the house," said Roger. "Just ain't got an extra bedroom right now."

"It's fine," smiled June. "At least this way I'm close to the horses."

Roger nodded. "I'll let you get settled. You need anything, you come on up to the house, just come in. I'll get you a key too."

"Okay. Thank you again."

June watched him leave then went to unpack her car. There wasn't much but she'd been determined to start over here. Smiling to herself, she grabbed her cowboy hat and put it on, checking herself out in the mirror. It was still fairly new but it would be broken in sooner rather than later.

Humming to herself, June put her few things away and hung up a picture of her father. It was the one thing she'd done in every place she lived, city or country. Smiling, June looked around and headed back outside.

Harlan was still working the paddock. She walked over to watch, leaning on the fence. He had a sure hand, which was always important when dealing with horses. He ignored her presence, keeping his focus only on the horse. June had done her research and she knew that Harlan was one of the best in the area, which was the other reason why he worked for his grandfather. Hopefully he didn't feel overly threatened by her being here.

After a while, Harlan finished what he was doing and looked at her. She was caught by his blue eyes, seeming to peer into her. His brown hair was just a bit on the long side, hanging underneath his hat.

"Suppose I should introduce you to the rest of the herd," he said.

June smiled. "I'd like that."

Harlan nodded and clucked at the horse he was with, walking it towards the corral. He pointed out each horse and gave their name and a little bit about them. June listened closely, not only because it was important to know, but because he had a gravelly voice that kept her attention.

"Then there's more in the barn," he said, leading her that way. "You've got the bunkhouse, yeah?"

"Yep. So I'm close to the barn if there's ever any need in the middle of the night."

"Not too often, but I have to admit I'll be glad for it. I've slept in the loft a time or two." Harlan got the doors and June stepped inside, giving her eyes a chance to adjust.

"Your grandfather has a lot of horses, doesn't he?" she asked as they moved deeper, the smell of hay and horses comforting and familiar.

"Yeah. We've been working this land since at least his grandfather was a boy. We've always been horse people. What about you? He said you've got experience, and I can see that you're rusty, but you've got some." Harlan was looking her over.

June ignored the slight barb. "I grew up in a place like this. Not this big, my father only had a couple horses. But he taught me most of what I know. And what I don't know I learned on my grandparents place. It was more this size, though still not as big."

Harlan nodded and led her down the stalls. He pointed out which horses were new and which ones were pregnant. "We've got a couple pretty good studs in the area, though he doesn't always use them."

I'll bet you have some good studs, thought June, then mentally smacked herself for the thought. They were coworkers and more than that, he was the boss's grandson. "Does your father work here?" she asked instead.

Harlan shook his head. "My dad left when I was young. Roger is my mom's grandfather. She lives in town, handles some of the business side of things."

"Oh. Sorry to hear that. My dad raised my pretty much by himself."

Harlan looked at her, maybe with a little more respect in his eyes. "You seem to have done all right for yourself.

"You too."

Harlan cracked a slight smile at her and took her out to meet the foals.

Eventually, they ended up back at the house for supper. She was a bit surprised to realize that Roger had cooked for them, but quickly covered it up. The food was plain, but filling. He smiled at her as she ate. "I'm too old to go chasing stallions," he said with a smile, "and I like to cook, sometimes anyway. Keeps me busy."

"Well, it's a great place you've got here. I can see how well you take care of your stock."

Roger scooped her another bit of potatoes. "They're good horses and I know I can trust Harlan to take care of them for me. And that's why I hired you, getting to be just a little more than one person can handle."

"I'll do my best not to let you down, sir."

"No, I am certain that you won't." Roger said, giving her a wide smile....

To continue reading search for 'The Ride of Her Life' by Kathleen Hope on Amazon.com

Extra Bonus Sample: Flames Of Passion

Amelie tapped her red Prada pump against the Coffee Shop's black tile. Her long, beautiful legs were crossed and a cloth napkin lay delicately on her thick thighs. She rolled her pretty blue eyes as the clock passed another minute after the time Mona said her blind date would be there. An annoyed sigh escaped her beautiful, thick blood-red pouting lips, and she twirled her long blonde hair as a woman came through the coffee shop door. Amelie looked out the window and decided to leave. The next person to come through the door was a shorter man with a muscular build. He had fire red curly hair and a baby face that was covered in freckles. Scars from burns also plagued his face. Amelie cringed as he sat down at her table.

"Hello, my name's Parker Moore. You must be Amelie Rose. Mona told me all about you, but her words couldn't do your beauty justice." He said extending his hand, it was also burned and hard for Amelie to look at. Amelie scoffed back and denied his extended over work worn, permanently stained and callused hand. She knew he was the firefighter Mona had told her about. Some friend she was. Mona knew that this man wasn't the kind Amelie was interested in. Her last three boyfriends owned islands and paid for them with modeling jobs.

"Ugh, yeah. I think Mona was mistaken though, I'm afraid I'm going to have to cancel the date." Amelie said as she stood up and straightened her designer black dress.

"If this is because I was late I'm so sorry. I got called into work, it was an emergency. I got here as soon as I could. I really would like to apologize properly if you'd allow me to." Parker stumbled on his words, extending his gnarled hand again. The fear of rejection hung in his bright emerald eyes, but he smiled.

"I'm sorry. It's not your timing." Amelie said as she left the coffee house without taking another look at the unattractive man. Amelie watched through the window as Parker sat himself down at the table and held his heavy head in his arms.

Amelie continued down the street picking up her phone. As she called Mona she prepared herself to scream at her for her betrayal.

"I can't believe you would set me on a date with that monster of a man." Amelie said as Mona answered.

"Amelie I told you that it was a favor for Bill. He just lost his wife and needs a confidence boost." Mona asked pleading.

"Is that what I am to you? A confidence boost?" Amelie hung up violently. Anger rose from within her. A favor to Mona's husband? How unbelievable.

This date was supposed to get her back out into the dating world. Amelie's last boyfriend, Nathan had left a horrible abyss within her that no amount of shopping could fill. This date was meant to be a distraction for her, not a favor to Mona's idiot husband Bill. Amelie fumed even more thinking about Nathan and the missed opportunity of a night off. She walked the streets of New York aimlessly, stomping her pumps. The ring of Amelie's phone almost made her jump out of her porcelain skin. She was happy for the chance to tell Mona where she could shove her blind date.

"Mona I don't want to speak to you right now. I can't believe you." Amelie said as she went to shut the phone again. A man's voice surprised her as it came through.

"Is this Amelie Rose, daughter of Raquel and Samuel Rose?" The man's voice sounded apologetic.

"Yes." Amelie said with extraordinary pride for her wealthy, successful parents. It was normal for newspapers and magazines to call asking for interviews about the corporate power couple.

"Miss Rose, I'll need you to come down to your parent's home at your earliest convenience. The sooner the better." The man on the other end of the phone hung up.

Amelie jogged to the side of the street and hailed a cab. She had the driver rush to her parent's home on Park Avenue. Thoughts of what awaited her when she arrived got her excited. She hadn't seen her parents in about two months and her twenty first birthday was just around the corner. Perhaps it was a surprise party or an elegant soiree she thought, hoping for something dazzling. When she arrived, she wasn't greeted by servers dressed tastefully, or acrobats on the lawn that were paid by her parents. There were no decorations or music either. Instead, she was greeted by grief and agony that struck her heart. There, the mansion that Amelie had grown up in was burnt down completely. Smoke hung in the still air above the house, and fire trucks were parked close as police officers talked to neighbors. Nothing but ash and rubble remained of her childhood home. She ran up to the gate where police officers and firemen stood talking, frantically looking for her parents. A woman with hair pulled up into a tight bun and a blazer walked up to her.

"Miss Rose, I'm so sorry to inform you, but there were no survivors of the fire. Your parents were inside the house when it ignited." Amelie's knees and purse hit the hard pavement and she let out a shrill scream as her entire world crashed around her.

People walked around her as she cried and cursed god. Mona's pearlescent Cadillac pulled into the extensive drive way and she ran to her dear, distraught friend. She knelt down next to Amelie and held her in her arms. Amelie cried as Mona rubbed her back and comforted her. It slowly became night and the sky turned black. Stars twinkled, not seeming to care about Amelie's crushed life. She still sat on the driveway in front what remained of her family's mansion and rocked herself in Mona's soft arms.

"Sweetheart, let's get you home. Here's your phone." Mona finally spoke as she helped her devastated friend up. She slipped a phone that was lying in the driveway into Amelie's handbag along with the contents that had spilled onto the driveway.

Amelie nodded as Mona helped her into her Cadillac. Bill silently drove Amelie and Mona to Amelie's apartment across town. None of them said anything, but Amelie did what she could to not look at Mona who was flashing her sympathetic big, brown eyes toward her. Amelie hated feeling pitied. It made her feel vulnerable and weak. She looked out the car's tinted window and did everything she could to not break down again. Her breath was hard to catch and she squeezed her eyes tightly. The tall white building with layered balconies appeared out the window and Amelie took a deep breath. The same place that Amelie called home for the past three years suddenly felt unfamiliar. She wanted nothing but her parents and her childhood home. She wished to go back and accept her mother's offer to live with them but remembered how she insisted to be on her own.

"Are you going to be okay tonight, dear?" Mona asked, putting a delicate hand on her back. Amelie left the car as she slammed the door and went into the apartment without responding. She didn't understand her anger toward Mona but she was glad to have somewhere to direct it. The Cadillac drove off into the night and Amelie wanted to scream at them not to leave her alone. Instead, she walked up the stoop and into the building, holding her head high.

Her luxurious apartment had never felt so empty and baron as she unlocked and opened the door. Amelie turned on the lights and took the single photo that hung off the hallway wall. She took it into her bedroom with her, holding it tightly. She passed an art easel with the same unfinished and untouched painting that had sat there for over a year. All the walls were white and it didn't really look like anyone lived there. There were no decorations or photographs besides the one in her trembling hand. She unzipped her black dress and let it fall to the floor before kicking off her pumps and threw her handbag onto the side of her bed. All that remained on her toned, tanned body was her red and black lace lingerie that Nathan had given her before she found him cheating with the elementary school teacher. She wished the underwear hadn't been so appealing so she could throw it away and forget about that asshole. She shook the thought of Nathan from her mind and crawled under the feather down Duvet and on top of the silk sheets and turned on the plain tableside lamp. She held the photo up to her chest and then looked at it. The photo was taken almost ten years ago today. It beautifully portrayed her parents and she on her eleventh birthday in front of what was now their charred tomb. Amelie let the hot tears streak through her carefully done make up as she remembered her wonderful childhood. She thought of the horseback riding she and her mother loved to do together and the golf she enjoyed with her father. Her heart was overcome by the feeling of guilt as she thought about all the time that had passed since she last saw her beloved parents. She ached inside to have that time back with them, that time to love and cherish them like they deserved. Amelie knew time was the one thing that she could never get back no matter how much money she had or how hard she worked. Pain and agony flooded her body; it was followed by the sensation that it was all a dream. The day had been so bizarre it couldn't have been real. The throbbing ache that Amelie felt was so severe, it couldn't be real. Sleep captured her to that thought, that none of it had happened....

To continue reading search for 'Flames of Passion' by Kathleen Hope on Amazon.com

Made in the USA
Middletown, DE
28 August 2019